I Am a

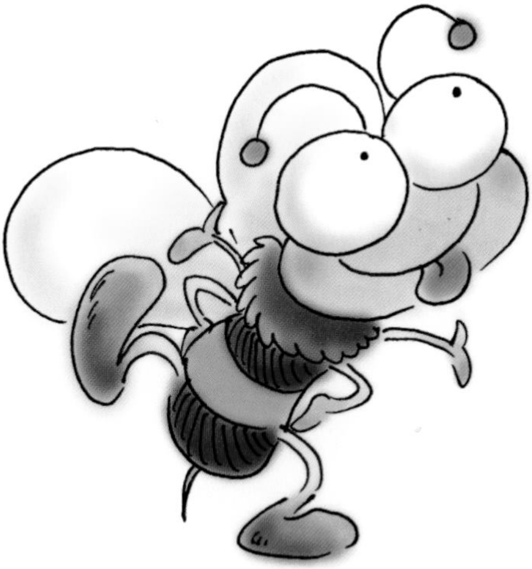

Illustrated by Stella Yang

Rigby

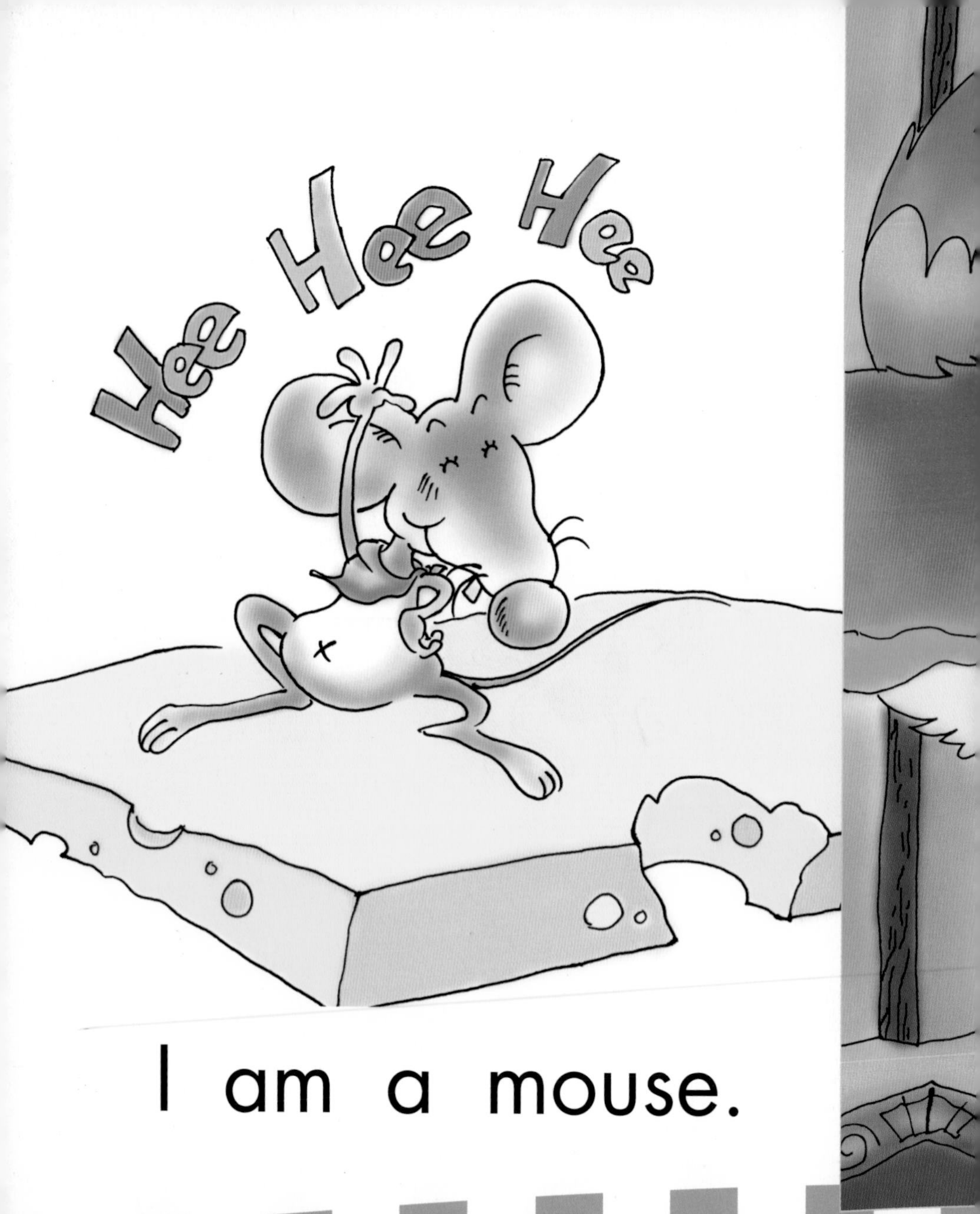

I am a mouse.

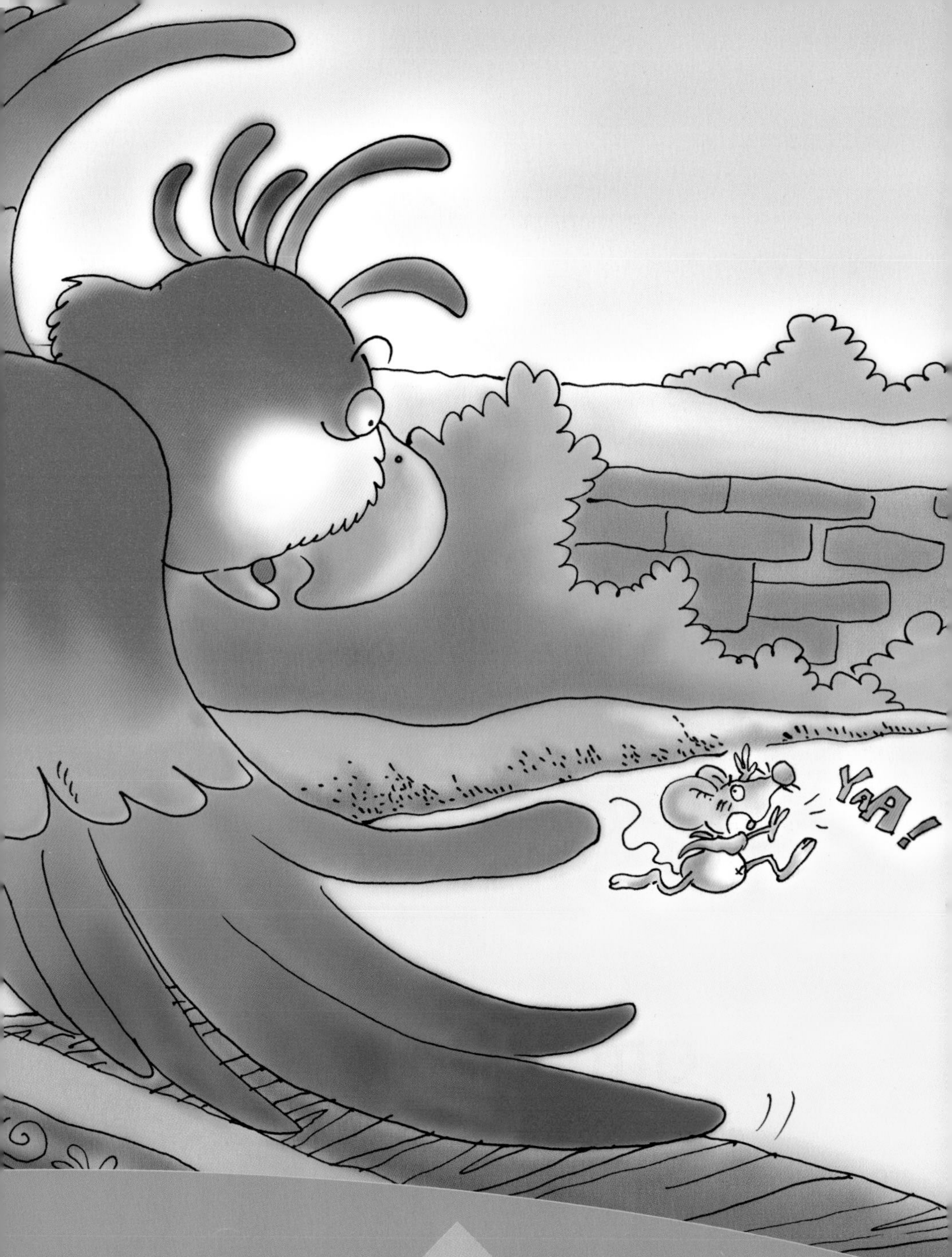
YaA!

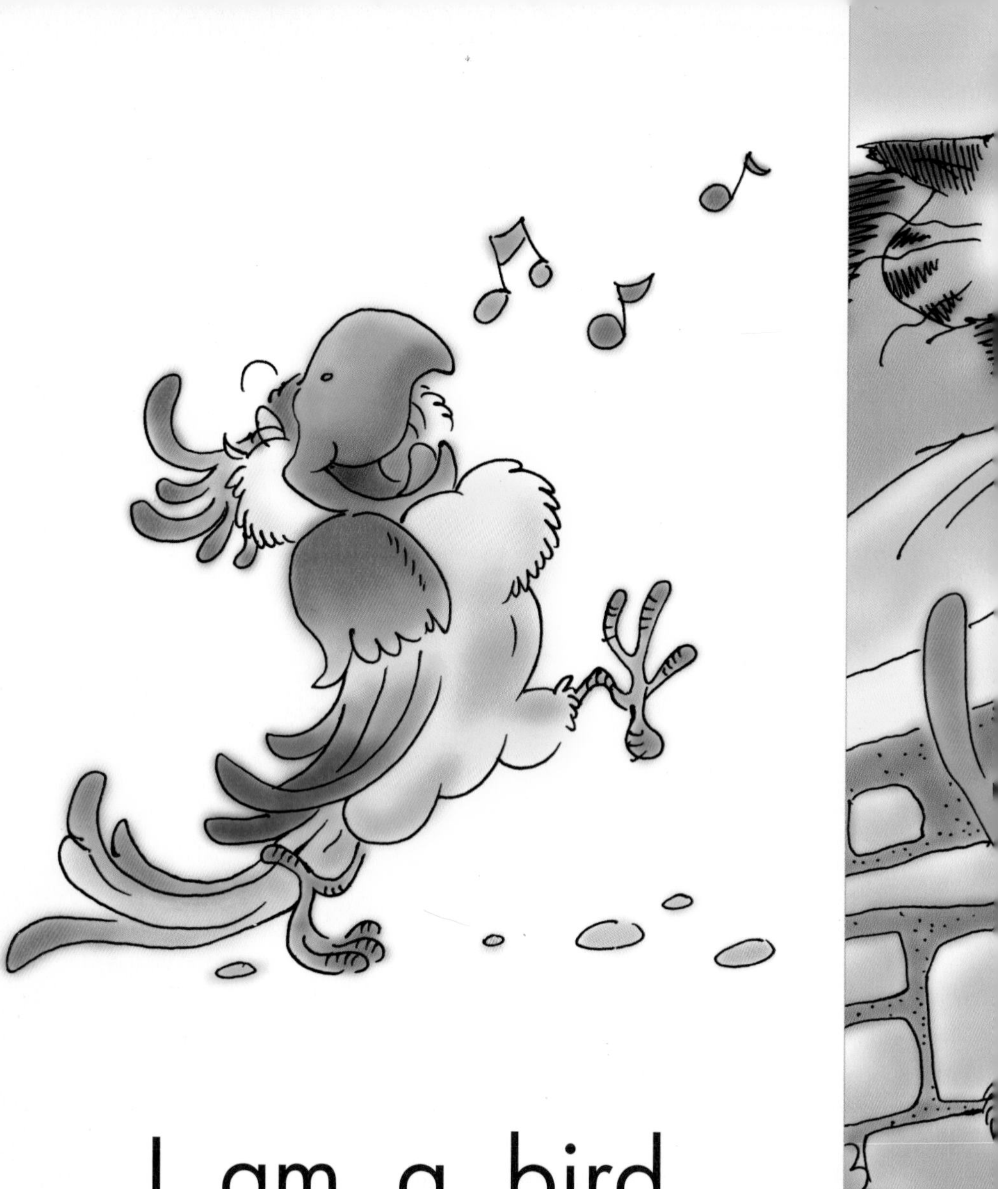

I am a bird.

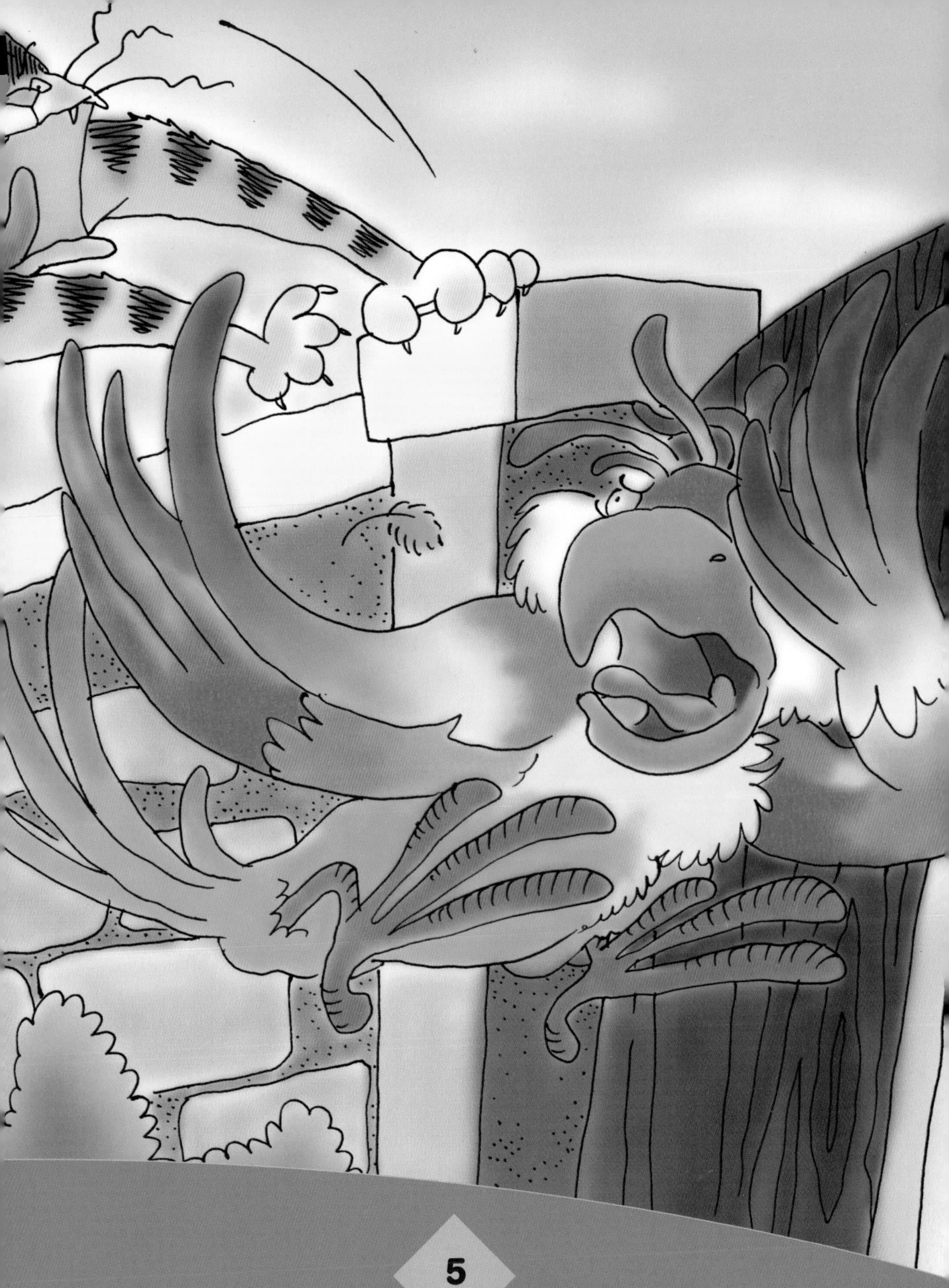

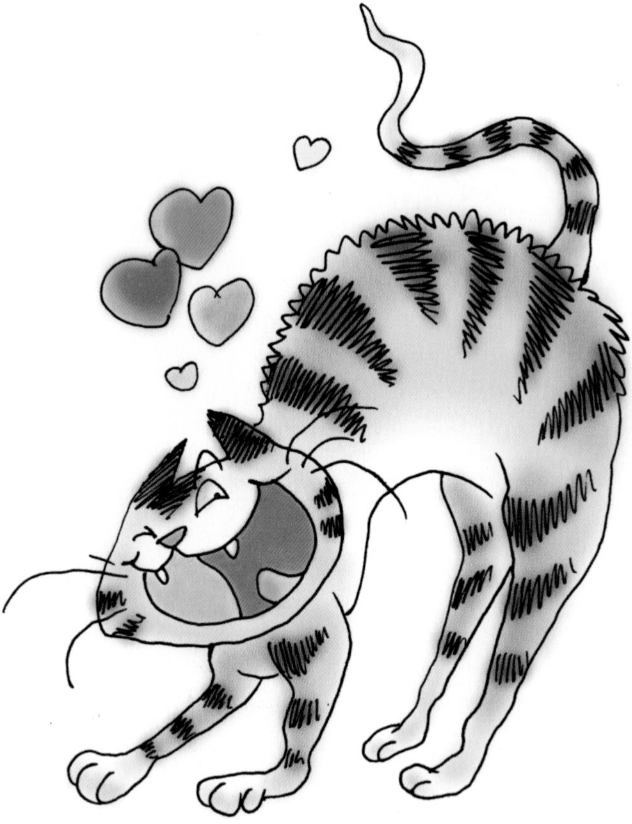

I am a cat.

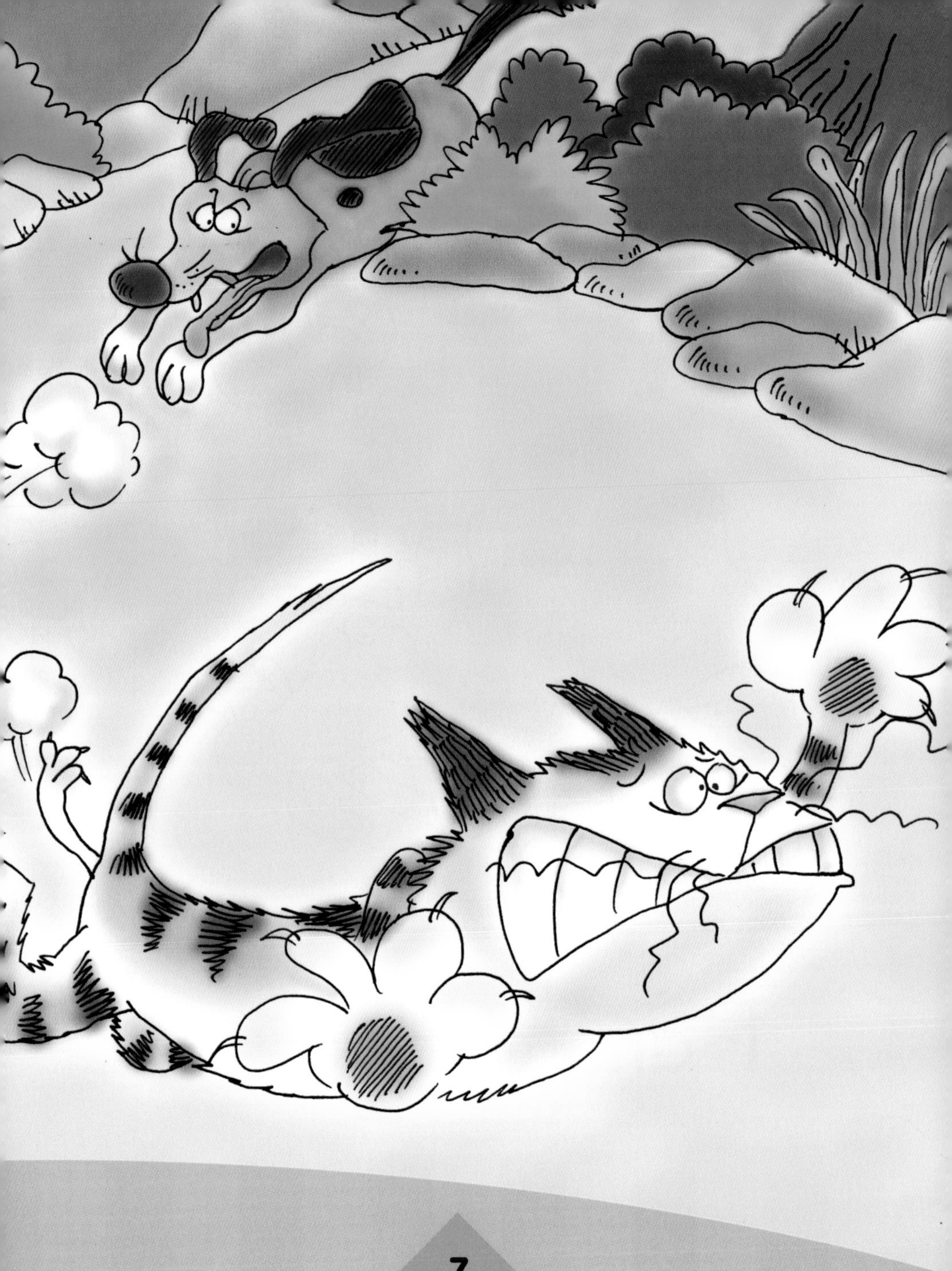

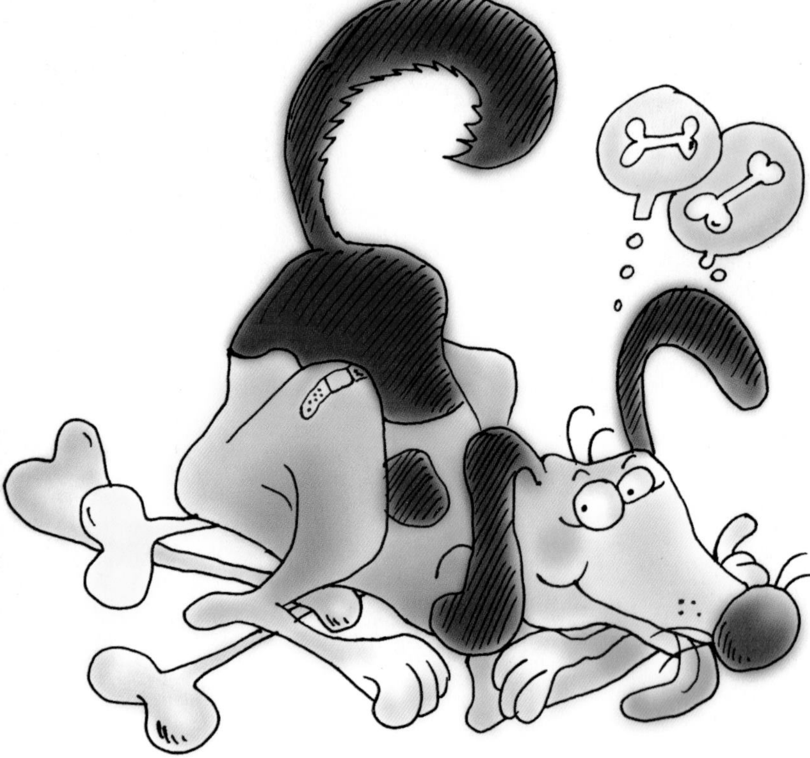

I am a dog.

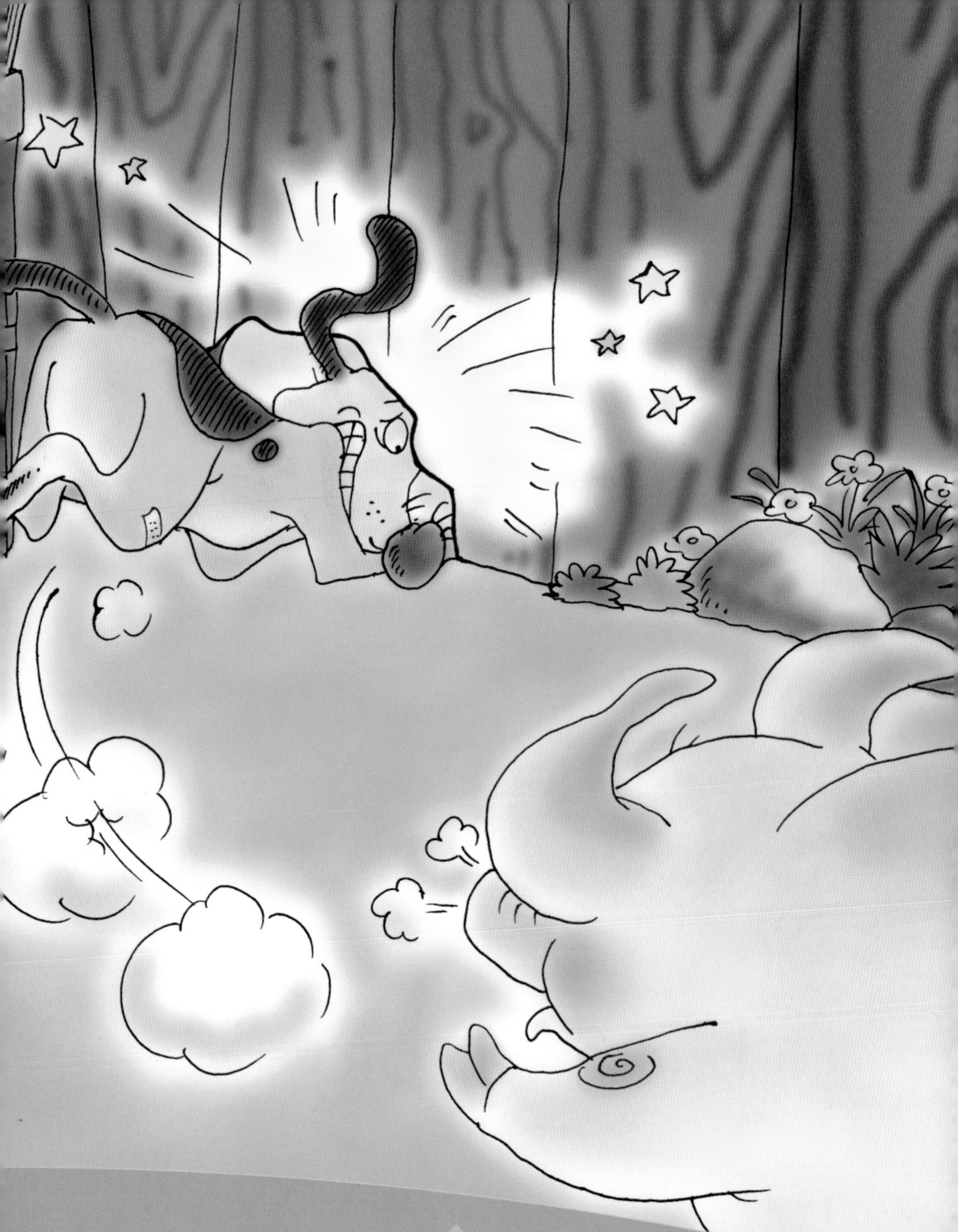

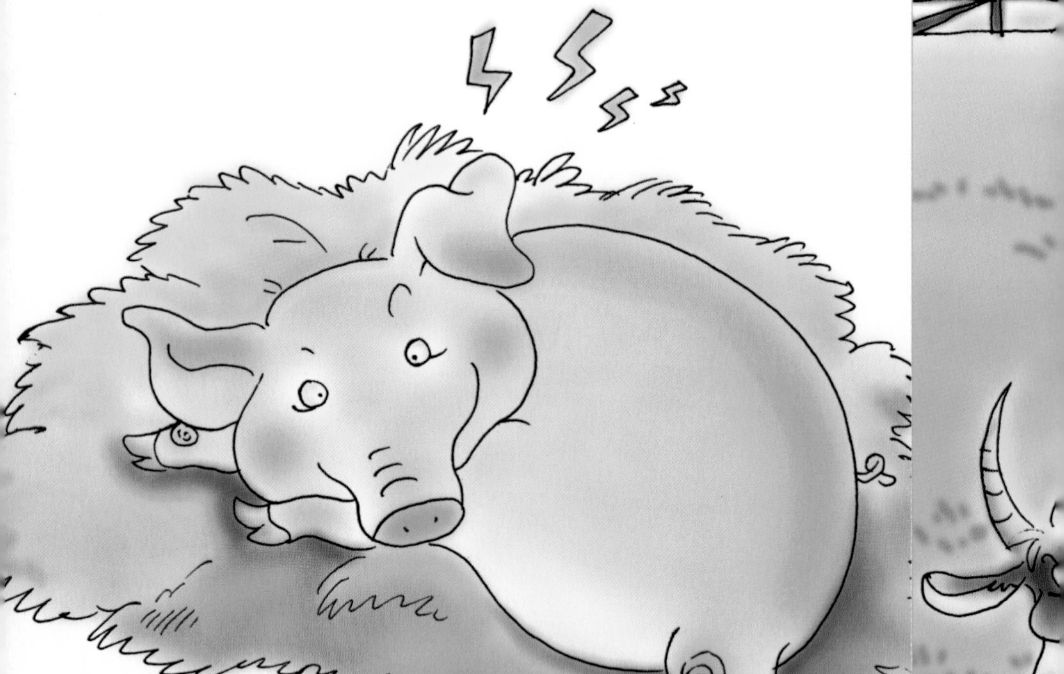

I am a pig.

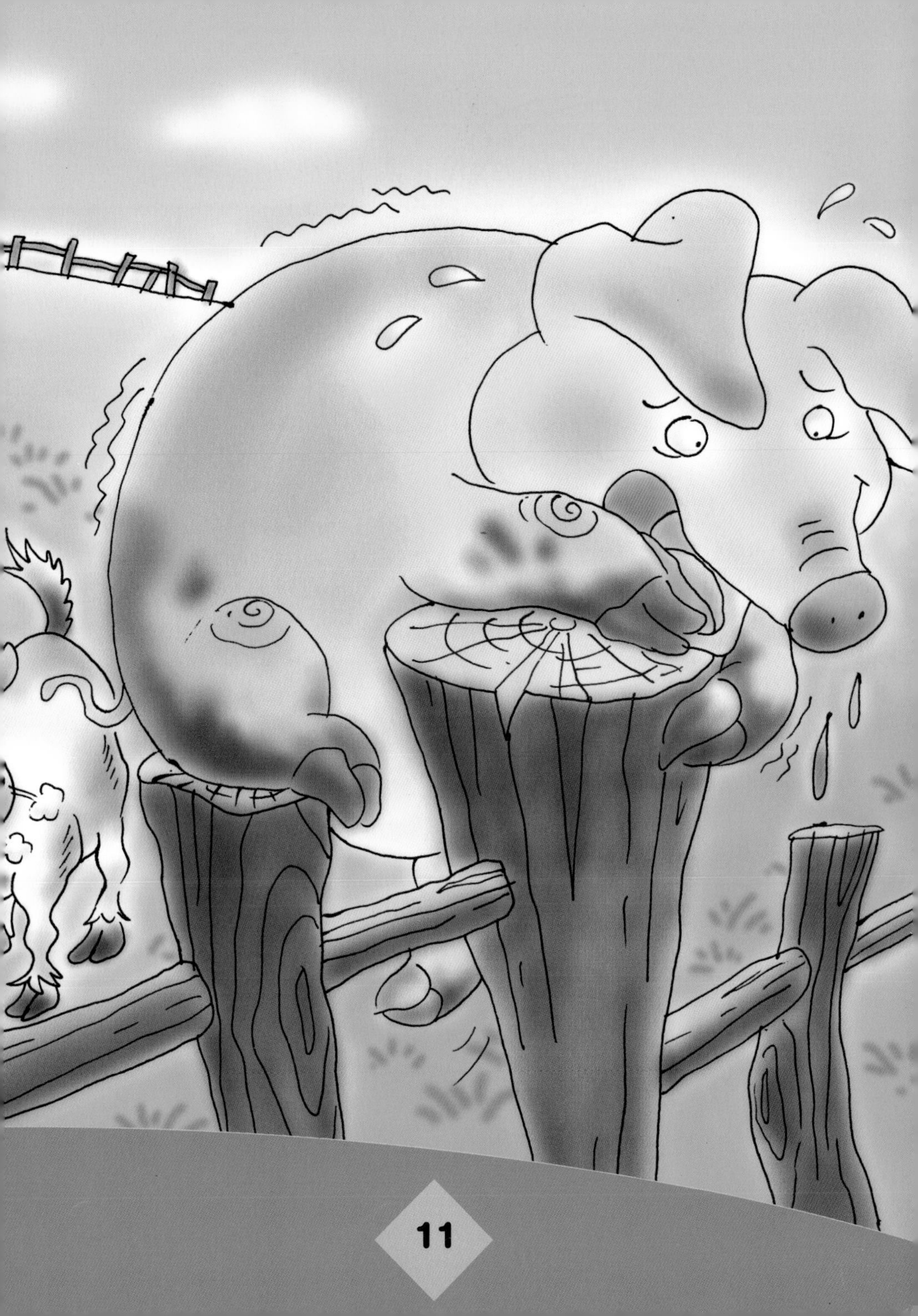

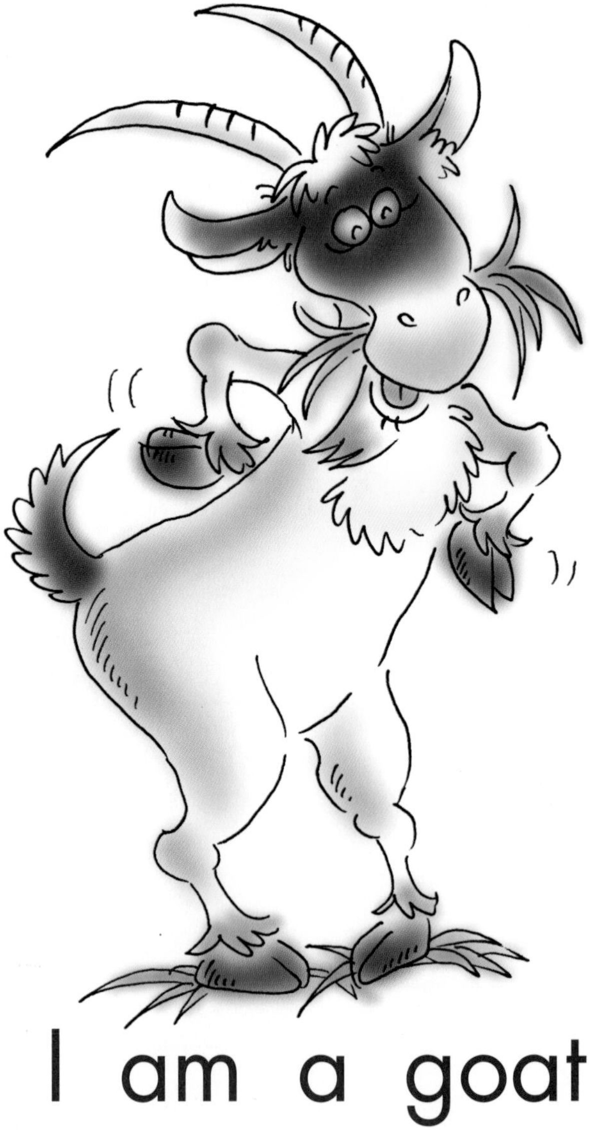

I am a goat.

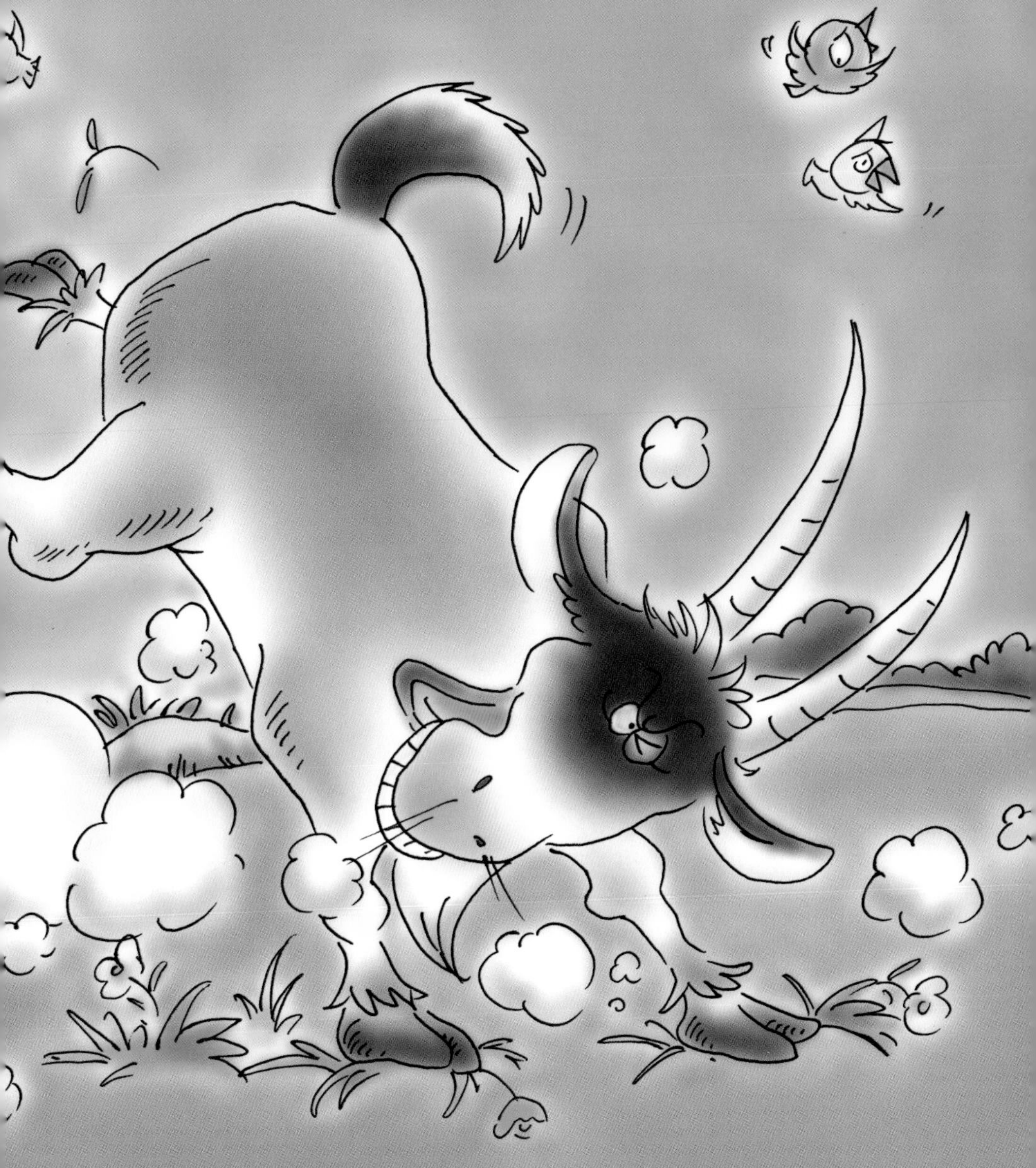

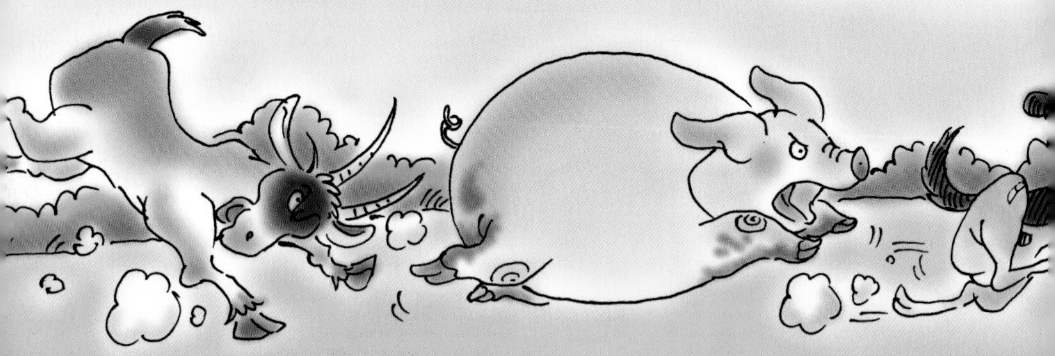

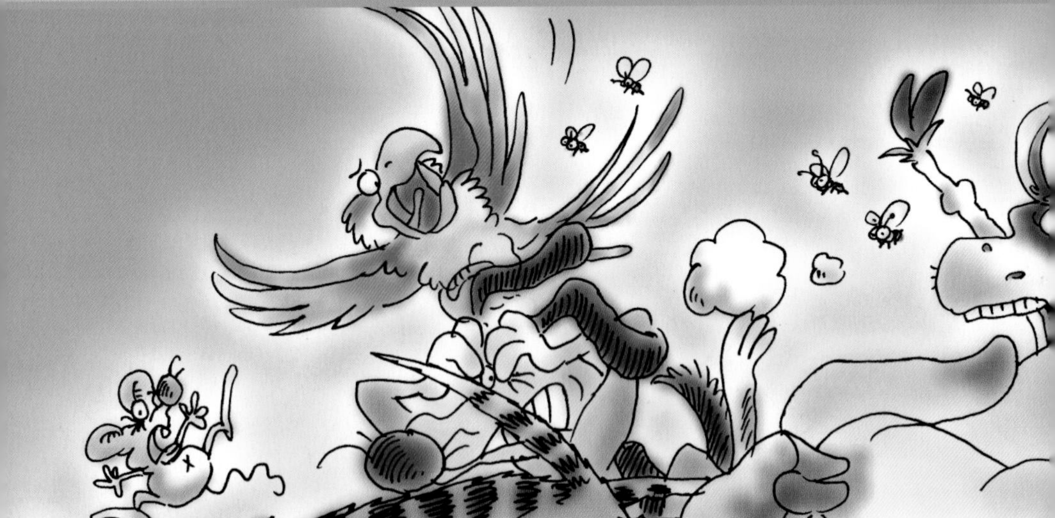

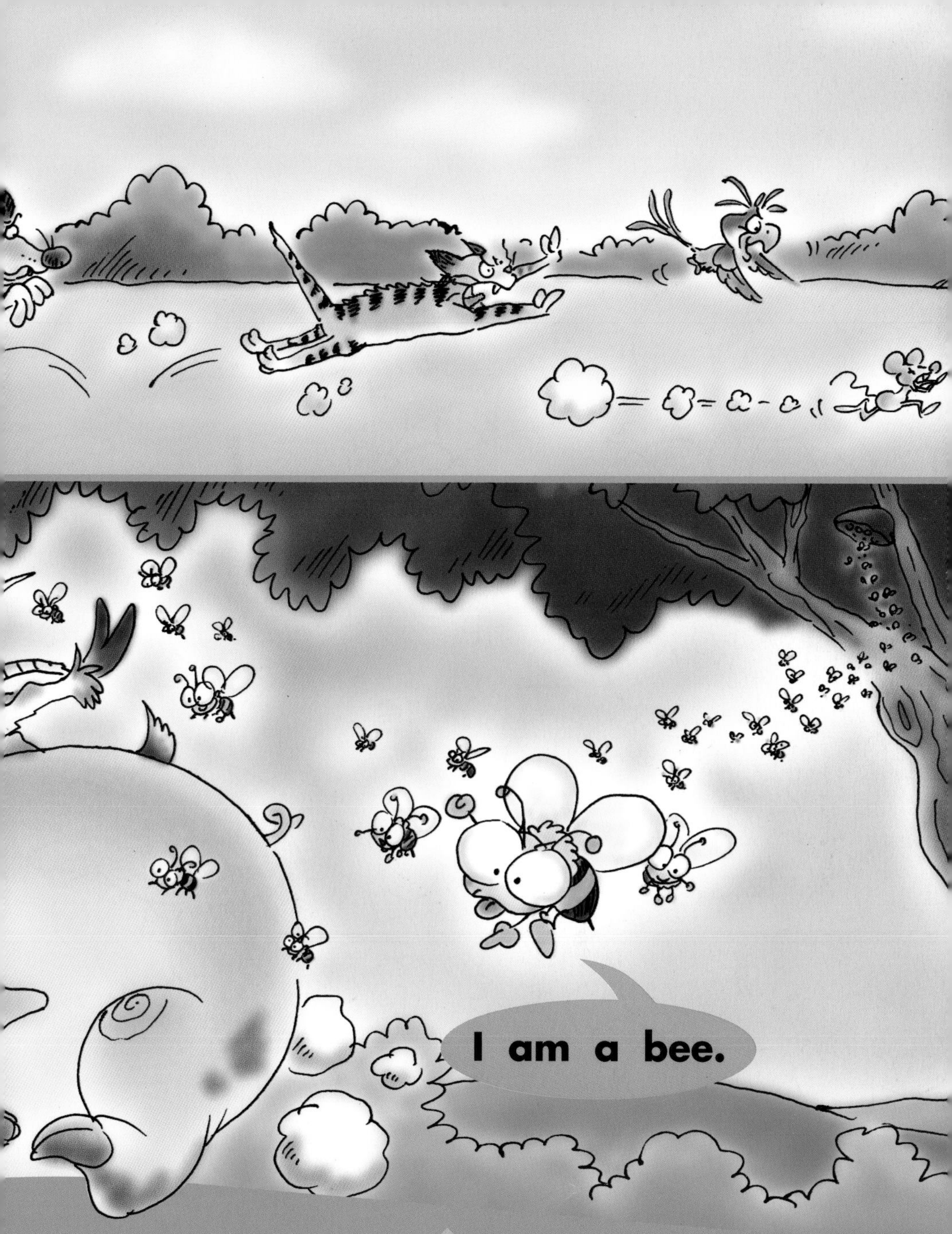
I am a bee.

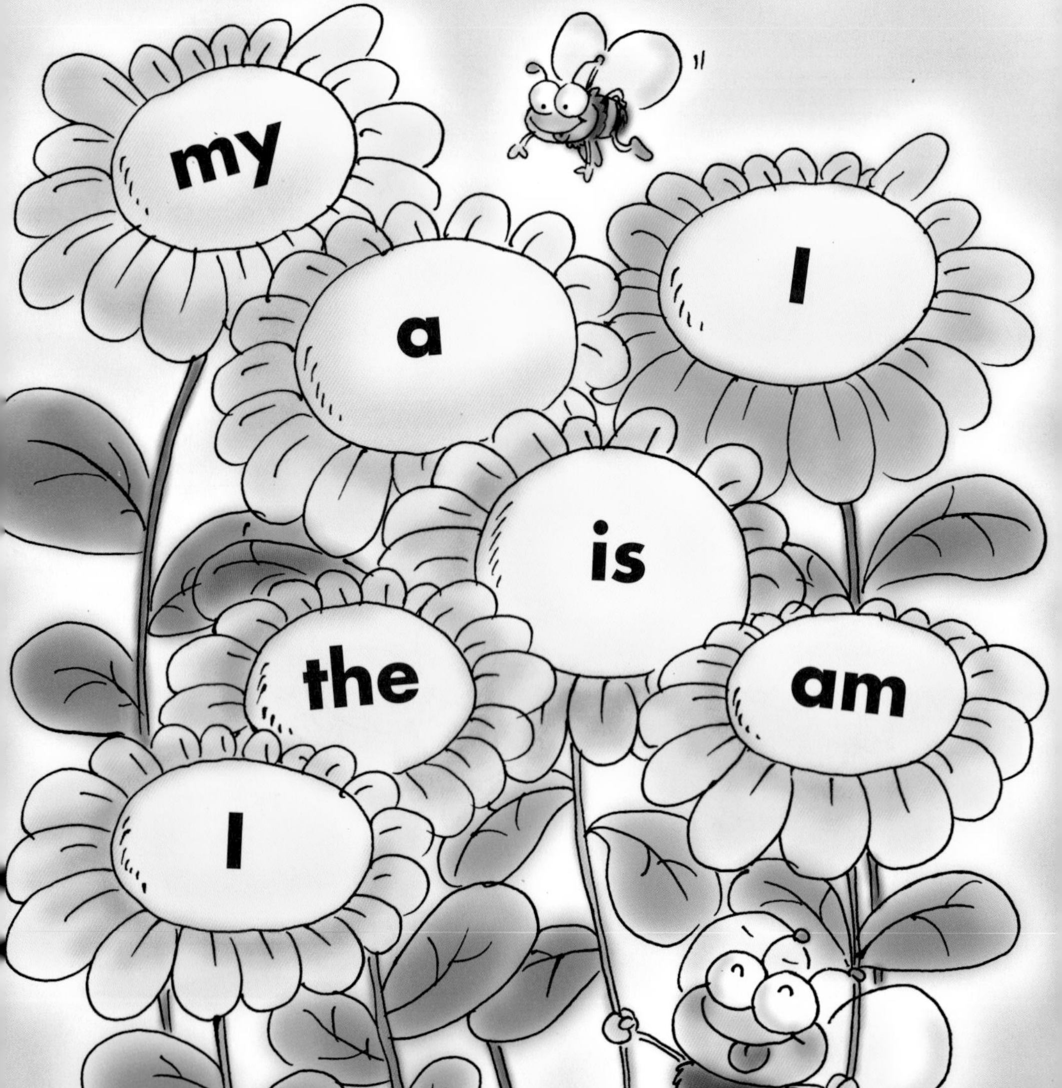
my
a
I
is
the
am
I